AFTER GOOD-NIGHT

AFTER GOOD-NIGHT

BY MONICA MAYPER
PICTURES BY PETER SIS

HARPER & ROW, PUBLISHERS

Library of Congress Cataloging-in-Publication Data
Mayper, Monica.
    After good-night.

    Summary: Nan stays awake to watch and listen until
everyone else in the house is asleep.
    [1. Night—Fiction.   2. Bedtime—Fiction]
I. Sis, Peter, ill.   II. Title.
PZ7.M47373Af 1987   [E]   86-45766
ISBN 0-06-024120-9
ISBN 0-06-024121-7 (lib. bdg.)

To my mother, my father
and Tom

After Good-Night

After good-night kiss and hug,

After Mama's one more story
and Daddy's Humpty-Dumpty song,

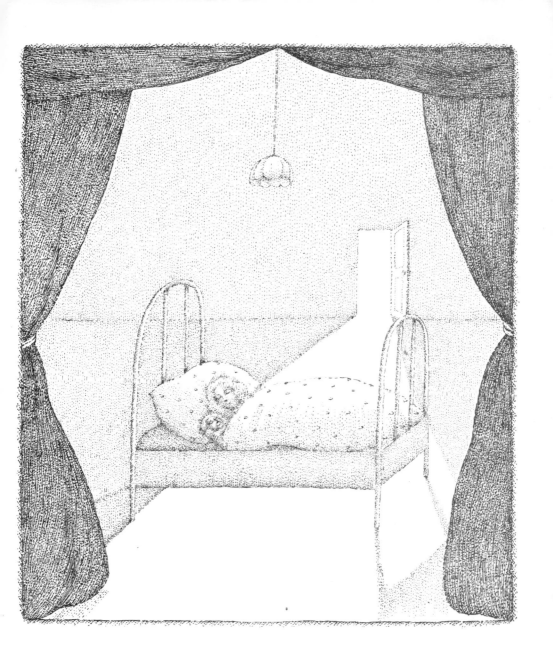

All Nan's bright light
shrinks to night light in the hallway.
Her family's soft night voices call,
murmur, hush and stop.

Brothers, two monkeys in their bunk beds,
one over and one under ...
Fast asleep.

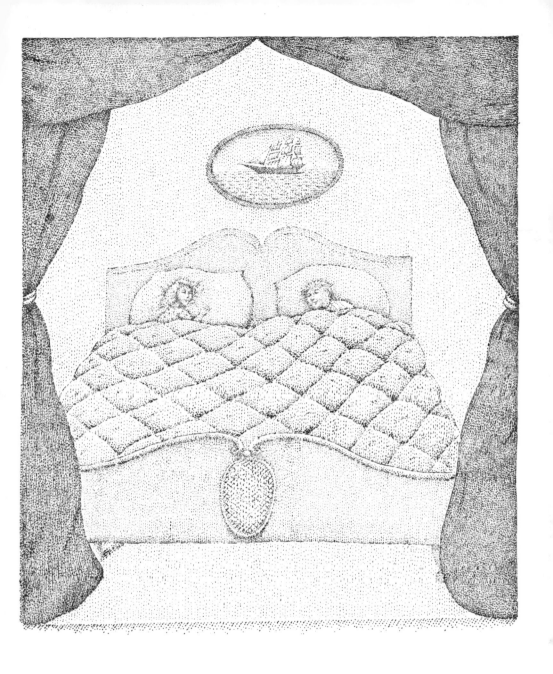

Mama and Daddy,
two bears deep in their warm cave bed…
Sound asleep.

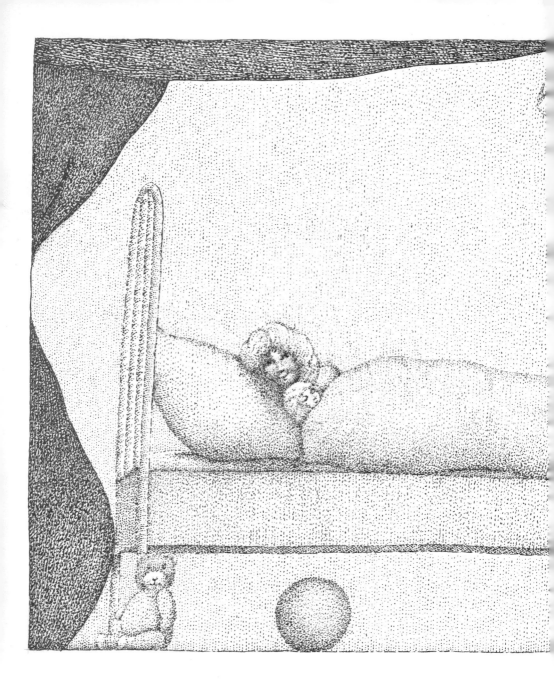

And Nan tucked into her own boat bed
with Pinky, tucked in tight...
All alone.
Wide awake.

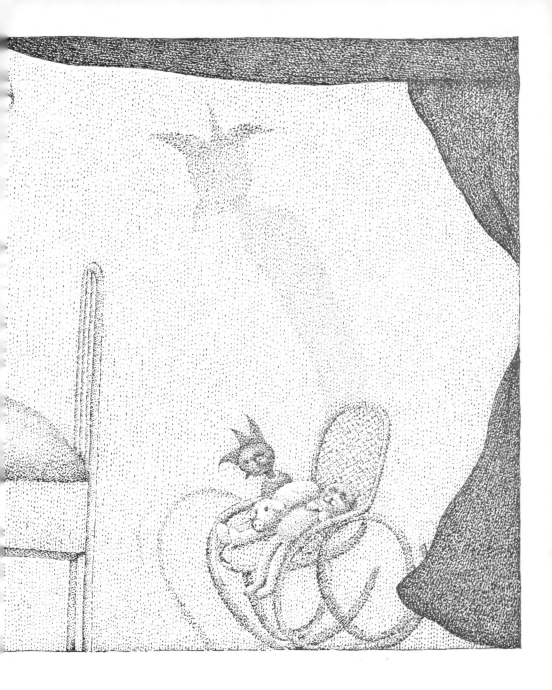

Nan is the eyes of the house:
The dark is dark-dark in the corner
where her chair has rocked
her animals to sleep.

The sky peeks in bright and blue-dark
at the edges of the window shades.

A web of passing car light
slides across the ceiling....
Nan holds her breath until it's gone.

Nan is the ears of the house:
Downstairs, the refrigerator hums and shudders.
Nan shivers close to Pinky.

A secret ocean hisses in the toilet tank.
The brass clock on the mantel
tocks and rocks and bongs....

Nine...Ten...Eleven...
Nan counts the bongs for Pinky.
She hears her brothers breathing,
one over and one under...
Fast asleep.
She hears her cave-bear mother snore:
Sound asleep.

She hears
her father's footsteps—
He's up and on his night walk,
checking the front-door lock,
winding the brass clock,
jiggling the toilet handle,
till Nan's secret ocean fades.

He tiptoes past Nan's doorway,
a shadow in the night light.
Nan breathes her own good-night
tucked in tight with Pinky...
Half asleep.
Shhhhhh.

The night wind bellies out the curtain,
and Nan's bed-boat sets sail.
Nan and Pinky
Lift
Drift
Turn

And turn again.

Nan is the eyes, half-closed eyes,
of the night—
Hush.
Over her, the stars shine steady in the blue-dark.
Nan is the ears, half-listening ears,
of the night—
Shhhhhh.

Under her, the wind whispers
down into the tree trunks.

She sails on in her night boat—
Lift
Drift
Turn.
Fast asleep

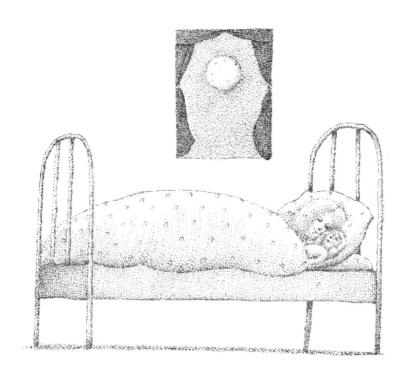

Sound asleep

Shhhhhh
Asleep.